# Treasures
## of the Snow

From the book by

# PATRICIA ST. JOHN

## SCRIPTURE UNION

© Scripture Union 2002
First published 2002

Scripture Union, 207-209 Queensway, Bletchley,
Milton Keynes MK2 2EB, England
Email: info@scriptureunion.org.uk
Web site: www.scriptureunion.org.uk

ISBN 1 85999 596 9

The pictures in this book are from the film *Treasures of the Snow*,
available on video from International Films, 36 High Street,
Princes Risborough, Bucks HP27 0AX.

Printed and bound in Singapore by Tien Wah Press.

British Library Cataloguing-in-Publication Data.
A catalogue record of this book is available from the British
Library.

**Design:** Mark Carpenter Design Consultants
**Photographs:** International Films 36 High Street, Princes
Risborough, Bucks HP27 0AX.

**Scripture Union is an international Christian charity
working with churches in more than 130 countries.**

# CONTENTS

# GLOSSARY

*alpine:* From the Alps, a high mountain range in central Europe.

*avalanche:* A slide of a large mass of snow or rock down a mountainside.

*chalet (sha-lay):* A wooden house with a sloping roof.

*chamois (SHAM-wa):* A small, sure-footed antelope that lives in the high mountains.

*crocus, primula, soldanella:* Different kinds of small, wild spring flowers.

*madame (muh-DAM):* The French word for "Mrs."

*monsieur (muh-SYUR):* The French word for "Mr."

*precipice (PRES-uh-pis):* A steep cliff.

*ravine (ruh-VEEN):* A deep, narrow valley worn by running water.

*Switzerland:* A mountainous country of central Europe.

*torrent:* A swift-flowing stream.

O ur story is set in a village high up in the mountains in Switzerland a long time ago. Annette Burnier and her little brother Dani live in a chalet with their father and grandmother. Their mother died when Dani was a baby. Annette is very fond of her little brother.

Lucien Morel also lives in the village with his mother and grown up sister, Marie, who works in a hotel.

Lucien does not like Annette. She does better at school than he does and he thinks she is stuck up. Annette does not like Lucien either. In fact Lucien does not have many friends.

"Grandmother," Dani announced, "I'm going up the mountain to pick flowers for Annette." It was the day before her birthday and she loved flowers.

Grandmother was not happy. "You are too little to go up the mountain alone," she said.

"Klaus will go with me. She'll look after me," said Dani. As if she understood what Dani had said, Klaus suddenly leaped into Grandmother's lap and began purring lovingly.

"Klaus is telling you that she will look after me up the mountain," said Dani, and picking up his kitten, he stumped off down the balcony steps, singing a happy song.

Grandmother watched the small figure heading towards the slopes with the kitten walking carefully behind him, until they were out of sight.

It was a beautiful spring day and the snowdrifts in the mountains were beginning to melt. The fields were bright with yellow and mauve crocuses, primulas and soldanellas. Dani wandered from one patch to another gathering flowers.

Klaus picked her way across the field until she reached the low stone wall at the edge of the field. On the other side of this wall was a rocky ravine with a rushing river at the bottom. Klaus sat on the wall and fluffed out her fur in the sunshine.

Dani loved beautiful things and in this field of flowers he was as happy as he could be.

Dani was so busy picking flowers that he never heard footsteps approaching until they were quite close. He looked up suddenly to see Lucien standing behind him with an unpleasant look on his face.

"Who are these for?" asked Lucien.

"For Annette," replied Dani.

"Well, I think your sister's a stupid show-off," said Lucien and, snatching the flowers from Dani, he trampled on them.

"I'll tell my daddy and he'll come to your house and beat you," shouted Dani.

Lucien was afraid of Dani's father. He wondered what he could do to stop the little boy. Then he spotted Klaus sunning herself on the wall and had an idea. He hurried across the field, picked up Klaus and held her over the edge of the ravine.

"Promise me you won't tell tales or I'll drop your kitten," he called.

Dani felt sick as he ran with trembling legs across the field to rescue his kitten from this bully.

Lucien never intended to drop Klaus but she suddenly struggled and gave him a sharp scratch.

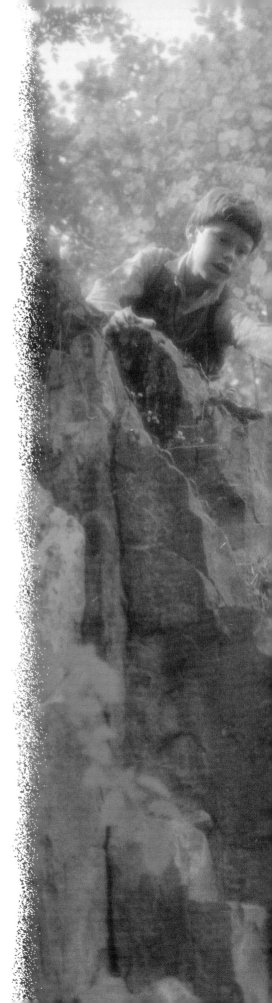

Lucien was taken by surprise and let go. Klaus dropped into the ravine just as Dani reached the edge. He gave a shriek and hurled himself after her before Lucien had time to grab him.

"Dani! Dani!" yelled Lucien. But there was no answer. Lucien believed Dani must be dead. He looked around wildly. No one had seen the accident. If he hurried home, no one would ever know he had anything to do with it. He ran home but he could not face his mother and instead he hid, sobbing, among the straw in the barn.

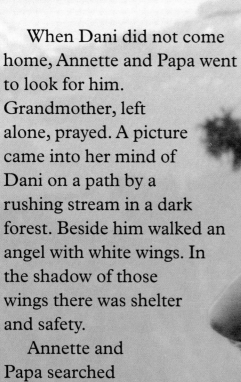

When Dani did not come home, Annette and Papa went to look for him. Grandmother, left alone, prayed. A picture came into her mind of Dani on a path by a rushing stream in a dark forest. Beside him walked an angel with white wings. In the shadow of those wings there was shelter and safety.

Annette and Papa searched the fields and up to the edge of the pinewoods, calling Dani's name, but the echoes of their voices and the sound of the rushing torrent were the only answers.

"I'll see if he's gone to Lucien's house," said Annette and ran off to Madame Morel's chalet while Monsieur Burnier went on into the woods.

Lucien's mother hadn't seen either of the boys. She and Annette went to look in the barn where they found Lucien, lying in the straw, crying bitterly.

"Lucien! Where's Dani?" Madame Morel demanded.

"Dani's dead... it wasn't my fault," Lucien sobbed.

"You must show us where he is - quickly," urged Madame Morel, dragging Lucien out of the barn.

Lucien set off up the hill as fast as he could go, sobbing all the time, with Madame Morel and Annette following him.

As they reached the wall
Monsieur Burnier appeared
from the woods and hurried
towards them. Lucien pointed
over into the ravine. "He's
over there, drowned in the
torrent," he whispered.

Dani's father looked over
the edge and saw a shivering
white kitten crouching on a
ledge.

He rescued Klaus and
then, securing his climbing
rope to a tree trunk, he
lowered himself down the
slippery rocks into the ravine
to look for Dani.

What he saw sent a rush of
hope to his heart.

Grandmother had been right. The angels had taken care of Dani and he had not fallen into the water but on to a boulder, where he lay with his leg doubled under him. Dani opened his eyes when his father hovered over him like a great big bird and then knelt beside him.

"Where is Klaus?" Dani whispered.

"She's safe. I'll carry you both home at once," replied his father.

He lifted his little son gently. Dani moaned because his leg hurt very badly. It was a long slow journey up out of the ravine. Dani's father could not climb the rope with his son in his arms. He had to scramble down to the edge of the torrent and then pick his way along to a place where the bank was less steep and he could make his way up.

Dani fell into a sort of sleep until his father laid him down on the grass. Annette put Klaus into his arms, where she purred like a little steam engine.

They laid Dani on a coat and Madame Morel and Monsieur Burnier carried him slowly down the mountain. Annette came behind carrying Klaus. It was a sad little procession and yet their hearts were full of grateful joy because Dani was alive.

No one, not even his mother, gave one thought to Lucien, who huddled miserably by the wall. When he found that he had been left alone, he felt as though they had all turned their backs on him. He got up, slunk home through the shadows and crept shivering to bed, feeling the most lonely and miserable boy in the whole world.

Dani lay in his bed feeling important because he had everyone's attention. He would have been very happy if his leg had not hurt so much. Annette sat with him until he fell asleep and then she went to wait with Grandmother for the doctor to come.

"Grandma, what shall we do with Lucien?" Annette asked. "He should be punished but I can't think of anything bad enough to pay him back."

Grandmother did not answer for a time. Then she said, "Have you ever thought, Annette, that when we do wrong it brings its own punishment? Think of how afraid Lucien must have been when he saw Dani fall and how miserable he must be tonight. Think of how afraid he must be of others finding out what he did. And then think whether he hasn't been punished quite enough already and whether we should forgive him and help him to start again."

Annette did not take much notice of Grandmother's words except for the bit about

others finding out what he did. She would make sure people in the village and at school *did* find out so that everyone would hate Lucien.

Suddenly there was a knock on the door and Marie Morel, Lucien's grown up sister, burst into the room.

"Annette, what's happened? My mother is so upset I can't get any sense out of her."

"Dani's broken his leg and it's all Lucien's fault. He dropped the kitten into the ravine and Dani fell in after it. In fact it wouldn't surprise me if Lucien pushed him."

Marie turned pale with horror. "I'll see that he's punished," she said as she hurried off.

Annette smiled. She felt that her revenge had begun.

The doctor sent word that they should bring Dani to the hospital, so next day Papa laid Dani on a straw mattress in the cart and they set off for the town. At the hospital, Dani was trundled off on a trolley and when he came back, his leg was cased in a white plaster. The doctor wanted him to stay there but Dani made a fuss and Papa decided to take him home.

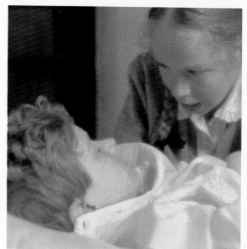

"I've got to wear these hard white trousers all the time," Dani told Annette and Grandmother when they arrived home.

Dani was put to bed on the sofa so that he could see all that was going on in the house. Annette came to sit by him. "Dani," she said, "you must promise me never to go near Lucien Morel again. You mustn't even speak to him."

At Lucien's house, Madame Morel scolded Lucien.

"If Dani is badly injured we'll have to pay all the bills and we can't possibly afford it. It's a terrible thing you have done. I hope you feel very ashamed."

Lucien was so ashamed that he didn't answer his mother at all. She saw that he had been crying in the night and felt sorry for him. "Now get ready for school and don't let the other children bother you," she said in a gentler tone.

Lucien set off for school and his mother watched him as far as the bend in the road.

He waved to her and then ran off up the hill as fast as his legs could carry him. He had decided he would hide in the woods all day.

In the peace of the forest Lucien felt safe. He sat down on a log, picked up a piece of wood and took out the knife he always carried in his pocket. He began to carve the shape of an animal and as he worked he forgot his misery and felt almost happy.

Lucien was so absorbed in what he was doing that he did not see the old man approach and was startled when he spoke.

"You carve well. Do you have any proper tools?"

"No, Monsieur, and I have no money to buy them."

"Come with me. I'd like to show you something."

Lucien followed the old man to his chalet further up the mountain. In the living room were shelves covered with carved wooden figures - bears and cows and goats and a host of other animals and people as well.

"It's a hobby of mine," explained the old man. "They keep me company on winter evenings. You've got talent. I'll show you how to use these tools and you can come here and carve when you want to. With a little training you might start to earn your living."

When Lucien arrived home, his mother asked him whether the schoolmaster and the children had said anything to him about the accident.

"No," replied Lucien shortly.

But then his sister Marie stormed into the house and the truth came out. The schoolmaster had met her in the street and asked her where Lucien had been.

Lucien sat in bitter silence. Everyone and everything seemed against him. Tomorrow he would have to go to school.

In class next day, when the teacher's back was turned, Annette wrote a note. She whispered to the girl sitting next to her, "Do you know what Lucien Morel did to my brother? He pushed him into the ravine. Pass this round the class."

The teacher saw the note being passed.

"Bring me that piece of paper. Is this your writing, Annette?" he asked.

"Yes, sir."

"Do you really think this is necessary?"

"But it's true, sir."

"I know. I find it difficult to understand what Lucien did but if I hear any more malicious gossip over this matter, I shall be very cross," the teacher said firmly.

At first the children chased Lucien and threw mud at him

but they soon gave that up and simply settled down to ignore him. When teams were picked he was always left till last. Lucien drifted into a lonely little world of his own. He walked to and from school alone, he shopped alone and in the playground he usually played alone. Even in the village, people rarely spoke to him.

Lucien looked forward to his visits to the woodcarver's chalet. Three times a week after school he bounded through the quiet pine forest and learned how to use the sharp knives and curved blades that were such a joy after his old penknife. He had decided to make a Noah's ark with tiny animals and to give it to Dani as a peace offering. Lucien was always thinking of Dani and he longed to ask Annette what the doctor had said. But Annette never looked at him or spoke to him and he dared not speak to her. Surely no one could give Dani a better present! And after that perhaps they might allow him to be just a tiny bit friendly with Dani again.

One day Lucien arrived at the old man's house with some good news.

"At school today they announced a handwork competition and I'm going to enter. I'm going to carve a horse. I'll show them I'm better than all of them."

"Oh, I'm sure you are. Why not use your Noah's ark?" the old man asked.

"No, it's a present for a little boy," Lucien said firmly.

"For your little brother?"

"No, he lives near me. He got hurt in an accident and can't walk."

"Oh dear, how did that happen?"

Lucien did not answer for a moment, but the fact that this old man had become friends with him and been so nice to him made him want to speak the truth.

"It was my fault," he said hesitantly.

I dropped his kitten over the ravine and he tried to get it."

As soon as he said it, he wished he hadn't, for he felt sure the old man would hate him now and drive him away like everybody else. But he didn't. Instead he said gently, "And are you hoping to make things right with this child by making this toy for him?"

"Yes," whispered Lucien.

"You are doing a good thing! It is hard work to win back love. But don't give up. If you spend time putting love into what you do for those who are not your friends, you will find happiness in loving, whether you are loved back or not."

When the Noah's ark was finished, Lucien set off with it to the Burniers' chalet with a mixture of hope and fear in his heart. Annette was sitting alone outside. Lucien walked up to her and held out the gift.

"It's a Noah's ark. I made it for Dani," he said timidly.

"How dare you offer presents to Dani!" Annette burst out. "Go away - and don't you ever come here again!"

And as she said it, she kicked the Noah's ark with all her strength into the woodpile

below her. All the little animals lay scattered on the logs.

Lucien stared at her for a moment. Then he turned and ran as fast as he could. All his efforts had been wasted. He would never be forgiven.

Then something the old man had said came into his mind like a tiny ray of light.

"Those who keep trying, find more happiness in earning love than in gaining it."

At least he had been happy making the Noah's ark. He wouldn't give up just yet.

Dani's leg was slow to heal but at last it was time to go back to the hospital to have the plaster taken off. Annette rushed out to meet the cart bringing Papa and Dani back. But to her dismay she saw that Dani had to be helped out of the cart and he had crutches.

"Grandma, look at the big hops I can do!" Dani announced proudly as he bounded up the steps into the chalet.

"Annette, Dani won't ever walk again properly. He'll always have a limp," Papa said quietly.

Dani thought of his crutches as a new toy and for some time he hopped about like an excited grasshopper. It was only when Papa said he was going to take his cows up to the high pastures that Dani realized that he could no longer follow the herd up the mountain. Then he sat down and howled loudly and could only be comforted by a promise that he could go up behind the herd in the cart.

Lucien told the old man about the Noah's ark.

"I'm sorry," the old man said. "I hope this doesn't make you want to give up now."

"I'll finish the horse for the competition," Lucien replied sadly.

Lucien spent hours over the horse and it was indeed a beautiful piece of work. Even his sister, Marie, admitted that it was good and when his mother saw it she said, "When you win the prize, they'll all want to be your friends."

Annette also had hopes of winning the prize. She had been knitting a sweater for Dani with a pattern of alpine flowers on a blue background.

"You're sure to win, Annette," her friends said.

It was the day before the competition and Annette passed by Lucien's house. On the steps leading up to the door some carving tools were lying and beside them stood the horse. Annette stopped in her tracks and gazed at the little creature. She realized it must be Lucien's entry for the competition, though he had never told anyone about it.

When she saw how good it was, she couldn't bear the thought that he would win the prize and be happy. He should not be happy if she could help it.

There was no one around. She reached out her hand for the horse, flung it on the ground and stamped on it. It lay in splinters. Annette walked home but somehow the brightness had gone out of the day.

29

When Annette reached her own chalet, Dani came hopping towards her excitedly.

"Look what I've found in the woodpile! There's a rhinoceros and a buffalo and a tortoise and lots more. I think the fairies made them, don't you?"

"Don't be silly, Dani," Annette said crossly. "I expect some other child dropped them - and you're too big to believe in fairies."

She turned away and went up the steps, hating herself for spoiling Dani's happiness. What had happened to her? But deep down inside she knew that she had done a mean, deceitful thing and her heart was heavy at the thought of it. She could not undo it. She ran upstairs to her bedroom and flinging herself on the bed, she burst into tears.

Lucien was looking forward to taking his little horse to the school competition. He went outside to collect it from the steps but it had gone.

"Mother, have you seen my little horse? I know I left it on the steps."

"Perhaps it has fallen over the railing," Madame Morel suggested. "Look down below."

Lucien's cry of disappointment brought both his mother and Marie running out and they stood gazing in dismay at the splinters on the ground.

"The wind must have blown it over and someone's trodden on it," said Marie. "I am sorry for you, Lucien. Is there nothing else you can take?"

Lucien said nothing except, "I'm going up the mountain."

His mother watched with a troubled face as he ran up the hillside and disappeared into the forest.

"Everything goes wrong for that boy," she said sadly. "Will he ever succeed in anything?"

## CHAPTER FOUR | *The old man's story*

I wish I could go right away and start all over again where nobody knew what I'd done, Lucien thought as he trudged through the forest. His eyes rested on the Pass that ran between two mountain peaks and led to the town in the next valley where Marie worked in a big hotel. He had crossed the Pass in summer when the sun was shining and the ground was covered in flowers. Now it seemed to him like a door of escape from prison.

As he left the wood, Lucien saw the old man sitting at the door of his chalet, gazing at the mountains across the valley. Lucien was quite close before he saw him.

"Ah, how goes the carving and when are you going to win that prize?" he asked.

"I'm not going to win the prize. My horse is all smashed. It fell over the railings and someone must have trampled on it."

"Oh, I am so sorry," said the old man gently, "but you could enter something else. That chamois that you carved was quite good."

"I did that without the proper tools and

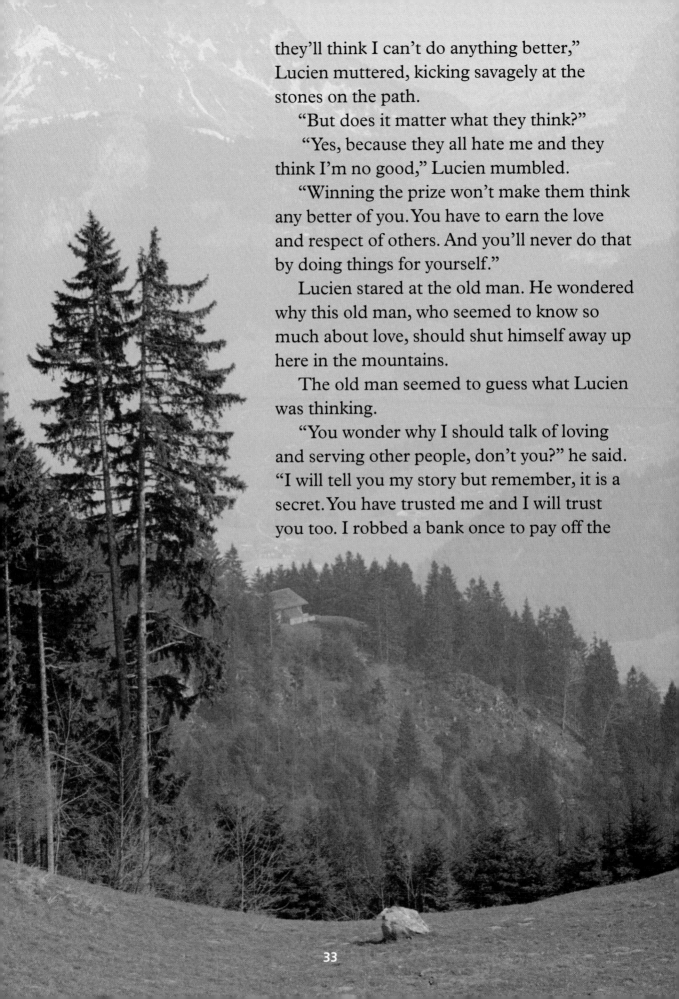

they'll think I can't do anything better," Lucien muttered, kicking savagely at the stones on the path.

"But does it matter what they think?"

"Yes, because they all hate me and they think I'm no good," Lucien mumbled.

"Winning the prize won't make them think any better of you. You have to earn the love and respect of others. And you'll never do that by doing things for yourself."

Lucien stared at the old man. He wondered why this old man, who seemed to know so much about love, should shut himself away up here in the mountains.

The old man seemed to guess what Lucien was thinking.

"You wonder why I should talk of loving and serving other people, don't you?" he said. "I will tell you my story but remember, it is a secret. You have trusted me and I will trust you too. I robbed a bank once to pay off the

debts I had from gambling. They caught me
and put me in prison. My wife had to look
after our two small sons. Then she became ill
and died. I think she died of a broken heart
and I had killed her. I passed the time in
prison carving and a kind warder used to take
my work and sell it. When I got out of prison I
came here to live."

"Where are your sons now? Don't they ever
come here?" asked Lucien.

"They don't know where I am. They are
grown up now and have good jobs. One's in
business and the other is a doctor. I don't
want to spoil their careers. I hear of them
sometimes from the man in the village who
sells my carvings. I have earned almost as
much money as I stole. I would feel much
better if I could do something worthwhile
with it. There... now you know my secret. I
hope it's safe with you."

It was the day of the handwork competition and the pupils and their families went to the school to see the entries and the judging. Annette, usually bright and talkative, was strangely silent as her friends ran to and fro, looking at the entries and chattering.

Lucien wandered round by himself, looking at the entries. He stared gloomily at the heavy looking bear made by Pierre, which everyone praised, and compared it with his own sprightly horse. He felt a stab of jealousy for Pierre who would now win the prize that belonged to him - Lucien.

Dani went to stand close to Annette's entry so that he might be right on the spot when the prizewinner was announced.

The teacher walked round slowly, picking

up and looking at the work. The room was so silent you could have heard a pin drop. Then a clear, distinct child's voice broke the silence.

"My sister made that," announced Dani. "I think it's the best, don't you?"

"Well, now that you mention it, yes, I think it is the best," answered the teacher.

"You've won the prize, Annette!" called out Dani and everyone laughed and clapped. And so, in this unusual fashion, the prizewinner for the girls was announced.

The teacher turned to the boys' entries.

"The quality of the work is very good but I have to confess that there is one which stands out above them all. The prize this year must go to Pierre."

Lucien went down to the village alone to collect the bread. As he walked back slowly up the hill past the school he wondered why he had felt brave yesterday about Pierre winning the prize but today he felt angry and jealous. The old man had talked to him about trying to become what God meant him to be, but it seemed impossible to change himself, however hard he tried. He was passing the corner where the path branched off towards Annette's chalet when he heard a child's voice singing.

He turned off to look and there was Dani with his kitten playing with something.

Lucien went closer and saw to his great joy that Dani was playing with the little animals that Lucien had carved for the Noah's ark.

"What are you playing, Dani?" he asked.

Dani jumped and his first reaction was to seize his kitten and say, "Go away!" But as he said it, he noticed how unhappy Lucien looked and he added, "I'm playing with my fairy animals but Annette said I'm not to talk to you."

"I won't hurt you," answered Lucien gently, "and I'm very sorry about your leg. That's why I made those animals for you."

"You didn't make them. I found them behind the woodpile," Dani answered and just then Annette called Dani to come for his supper.

Lucien turned away but felt more cheerful as he climbed the path home.

Dani hopped into the kitchen and climbed into his seat.

"Annette, Lucien said he made my fairy animals, but he didn't, did he?" he asked.

"I've told you not to talk to Lucien. He'll only hurt you again," Annette replied crossly.

"But I only talked to him a teeny weeny bit. Anyway, he didn't make them, did he?"

"Oh, do be quiet, Dani, and eat up your soup," Annette snapped and left the room before Grandmother, who was looking hard at her, could ask any questions.

Autumn came and went and suddenly it was Christmas. Annette and Grandmother were sitting in the kitchen together. Grandmother was knitting and Annette was thinking. Suddenly she said, "Grandmother, what does it mean when it says that Jesus knocks at the door of our hearts?"

"It means that Jesus sees that your life is full of wrong deeds and dark thoughts. He wants to come into your life and turn out those wrong thoughts and put his loving thoughts in you instead. It's like someone knocking on the door of a dark house and saying, 'If you let me in, I will take away the darkness and make it bright.' But remember, Jesus never pushes his way in. That is what knocking means. You have to say, 'Yes, Lord Jesus, I want you to come and live in me.' That's what opening the door means."

There was a long pause and then Annette said, "But if you couldn't stop hating someone, you couldn't ask Jesus to come in, could you?"

"None of us can stop ourselves thinking wrong thoughts, but if you ask the Lord Jesus to come in, it's like pulling back the curtains and letting in the light. The darkness goes when the light comes."

Annette did not answer. She did not feel that she could forgive Lucien, or tell him what she had done to his horse. She felt restless and decided to go out for a walk.

She wandered quite a long way through the soft snow and reached a little bridge over a

stream. The bridge was very slippery and
Annette fell and twisted her ankle.

She tried to get up but she could not walk
and she felt frightened because there was no
one around. She crawled towards a chalet up
the hill, painfully dragging her swollen foot
behind her. She called out but no one
heard her. She struggled up the
steps and knocked on the door.
There was no answer.

Annette
staggered up on
one foot and beat her
fists on the door, shouting,
"Monsieur Berdoz! Monsieur
Berdoz! Let me in!"

But nothing stirred in the house and she
realised it was empty. She sank down on the
steps and burst into tears.

She decided to wait a little and then try to
crawl back. As she sat waiting she thought of
something. She knew now what it felt like to
knock at a closed door and get no answer. She
had knocked for only a few minutes but the

Lord Jesus went on knocking for years - she knew he did.

Suddenly she heard a sound - the sound of skis running through soft snow. Someone was coming down the mountain. She knelt upright and shouted at the top of her voice.

"Help! Over here! I've hurt myself."

The skier turned swiftly and brought his skis to a stop. He unstrapped them and ran up the slope towards her. It was Lucien.

"Can't you walk at all?" he asked. "Look, here's my cloak to keep you warm and I'll go and get the sledge for you."

A moment later he sped off, feeling joy in his heart because he was able to do something useful for Annette. Annette, however, was left with plenty of time to think.

She closed her eyes. "Dear Lord Jesus, thank you for sending Lucien to help me. I'm sorry I've been shutting you out all these months because I wanted to hate him. Please come in now and help me to love Lucien."

Lucien came back with the sledge and reached out his hand to help her on to the sledge. She drew back. "Wait a minute," she said shakily, "I want to tell you something. You know that time your horse fell off the balcony? It was me. I did it on purpose because I didn't want you to win the prize. I'm sorry."

Lucien stared at her, too surprised to speak. But he felt very relieved, for Annette had also done something wrong. If he had to forgive her, perhaps she could forgive him, even though a smashed horse was nothing compared with Dani's leg. So he just gave a gruff little laugh and said shyly, "Oh, it's all right. Get on the sledge."

Lucien and Annette sped down the mountain and arrived at the Burniers' front door in a flurry of powdered snow. Annette climbed the steps and was met by Grandmother.

"Annette! What has happened to you? Papa has gone out looking for you."

"I hurt my foot but Lucien found me and brought me home," Annette said.

Grandmother saw Lucien standing shyly by the door. "Come in, Lucien," she said, "you're very welcome."

The door opened and Papa came in, shaking the snow from his cloak. He had seen the sledge whizzing across the fields. Soon he was putting cold bandages on Annette's swollen foot while Grandmother served out hot chocolate and crusty bread topped with a thick slice of cheese. They sat munching in silence and then Grandmother said, "Annette, I've tried not to interfere, but isn't it time you forgave Lucien?"

"I have - out on the mountain. I thought a lot about what you said about opening the door and I did it and it happened just like you said. And Lucien said he'd forgive me for something nasty I did to him, didn't you, Lucien?"

"Yes," replied Lucien and they smiled at each other.

Annette knew that she must go and see the teacher about the prize for the handwork competition. So, a few days later, she wrapped up in her handkerchief some of the little animals Lucien had made and went to his house.

"These are exceptionally good," the teacher said. "Why didn't he enter the competition?"

" He did,"Annette answered. "That's what I came to tell you about. He made a little wooden horse but I broke it because I was so angry about Dani. But I'm sorry now and I wondered if he could have a prize - now that you know about it."

The teacher looked at her thoughtfully.

"But I haven't got another prize. There were only two. One was given to Pierre and one to you."

"Well then, he ought to have Pierre's prize. His were much better."

"Oh no, we couldn't do that. After all, Pierre won quite fairly. If you really want him to have a prize you will have to give him yours. After all, it was your fault that he lost it, wasn't it?"

Annette sat thinking of the lovely book of pictures of the mountains in Switzerland that lay in her drawer and was the most precious thing she had. Of course, she could say no and the teacher would never force her to give it. But the Lord Jesus was living in her heart now and he wouldn't want her to keep anything back.

"All right," she said at last.

"Good!" said the teacher, knowing that Annette had won a big battle.

It was a happy day at school for Lucien. The teacher suddenly announced that he had seen such a good piece of wood carving in the holidays that he had decided to award another prize. To everyone's astonishment, Lucien was called out to receive it. All the children crowded round to admire the little animals and Pierre said it was lucky for him that they came in late or he would never have won the prize.

When they saw his prize, one of the girls said, "It's just like Annette's book."

"Is it really?" said Lucien and winked at Annette when no one was looking.

After school they walked back up the hill together.

"It was nice getting a prize but I think you ought to keep the book, Annette," Lucien said.

"No, it's yours now," Annette insisted.

"Well, why don't I have it this month, and

"And we'll change every month," replied Annette, feeling happy that she could still enjoy the book.

They sat down on a woodpile to look at the book together and Lucien, who was keen on mountains, pointed out to Annette the different ways of climbing them. They forgot about the time until a little voice said, "Annette, Grandma said I could come and meet you because dinner's ready and I've had mine."

"Dani! You shouldn't have come so far. We must go home at once."

Dani was very tired because he had never been so far alone on his crutches before. In the end Lucien carried him home.

## CHAPTER SIX | *Lucien's adventure*

Lucien went home to his chalet, thinking. The sight of Dani made him sad. Annette had made things right with him but he could never make Dani's legs right. He wondered why Annette had forgiven him and become so different. She had talked about opening a door to Jesus and now she was a much kinder person. It made Lucien think that Jesus was not just someone who lived a long time ago in Bible stories but someone who could really do things now.

Lucien went over to the cowshed and climbed up into the hayloft where he had hidden and wept so many months before. He did not understand what it meant to open the door to Jesus but he prayed with all his heart that God would heal Dani and make him walk properly again, as he healed people in the Bible.

When he came back into the house it was snowing hard and Marie burst through the door.

"There's a blizzard out there," she panted as she shook her wet clothes. "I had a real fight with the wind getting up the slope."

As they all sat down to supper together, Marie tossed a coin on the table and Madame Morel exclaimed, "What's this for?"

"It's a tip from a Monsieur Givet who's staying at the hotel. He's got a hospital down by the lake and he's very clever. He can cure almost anyone with broken bones."

Lucien leaned across the table excitedly. "Marie, could he cure little Dani Burnier?"

"Oh, I would think so, but have you any

idea how much it would cost? They'd never have the money."

"But would he just come and have a look at Dani?" pleaded Lucien.

"He leaves tomorrow - early. Anyhow, the last train went hours ago and the road over the Pass would be blocked on a night like this. Stop worrying about Dani, Lucien."

Lucien said no more but his thoughts flew to the old man up the mountain who had plenty of money. He would try.

After supper Lucien went to his room, put on his woolly hat and cloak and his strongest boots. Then he wrote a note to his mother telling her he would not be back till morning.

He went across to the barn, took his skis and a storm lantern and set off for the old man's house. His great adventure had begun.

Lucien reached the wood and went up through the tossing trees until he could see the orange glow of light in the old man's window. He knocked on the door.

"Who's that? My boy, what brings you here in this weather?"

Lucien sank down on the bench to get his breath back, then he looked up into the old man's face.

"You know you once said you were saving your money to give to something worthwhile? If you will give me your money, I think little Dani's leg might be made better."

"How could that be?" asked the old man.

"There's a doctor at the hotel where my sister works who can mend broken bones. I'm going over the Pass now to ask him to come and have a look at Dani, but my sister said he'd want a lot of money."

"You must be mad, boy! You couldn't cross the Pass in this weather."

"I think I could on my skis. The fresh snow won't be too deep yet if I hurry. But it's no good going unless I have the money."

"But can we be sure the man won't cheat us? What is his name, Lucien?"

"My sister says he's a very famous man. His name is Monsieur Givet."

"Monsieur Givet!" said the old man softly in a strange voice. But he turned away and opened a little cupboard. He handed Lucien an old sock stuffed with notes.

"Take it all and give it to Monsieur Givet. Tell him it is the payment of a debt. And don't tell him about me or where I live."

"Thank you very much. I'll give him your message."

Lucien sped off as fast as he could through the soft snow. At the edge of the wood he turned and waved his lantern. Through the whirling snow he could see the outline of the old man against the light from his open door.

He skied down over the meadows and through the deserted village to the lowest part of the valley. Now he must carry his skis and climb up over the Pass that ran between the two mountains. He climbed through the woods for three hours, his mind full of the horrors of all the dangers that were to be found on the mountains - avalanches, treacherous snow drifts, falling tree branches. He was not even sure if he was on the right path. If he wasn't, it might lead to a precipice. He found his teeth were chattering and he was crying.

"I'm so frightened. I can't go on," he sobbed to himself. And then he suddenly remembered that afternoon when he and Annette and Grandmother had sat together in the warm kitchen. Grandmother had talked about being afraid. "Perfect love drives out fear... if we believe that Jesus loves us perfectly there is nothing to be afraid of."

Lucien realised that he was not alone after all. It was as if someone stronger than the wind and the darkness had suddenly come and taken his hand and pointed up the mountain. Lucien went on.

"Perfect love drives out fear... help me, God," he murmured over and over again.

He struggled on, bent nearly double. One icy blast knocked him onto his back and he hardly had the strength to get up again. At last the ground started to slope gently downwards and he knew he had crossed the Pass.

He buckled on his skis and zig-zagged carefully through the trees on the forest track.

When at last he glided out into the open, the fields lay silver in the moonlight and the dark town was below him.

Monsieur Givet woke very early and remembered that he was going home today. He had just finished shaving when the night porter knocked on the door of his room.

"Excuse me, sir, were you by any chance expecting a visitor?"

"A visitor? At this hour and in this weather?"

"Yes, it's like this. About a quarter of an hour ago I heard a little tap on the door and when I opened it there's this boy on skis, white as a sheet and looking more like a ghost than a boy. 'I want Monsieur Givet,' he said and then sank down on the step and leaned his head against the doorpost.

'Well,' I said to him, 'you can't come calling on people at this time of the morning - he's asleep in his bed.' 'Then I'll wait,' he said and his head sank down to his knees. I took off his skis and dragged him inside and put him on a chair. 'Where have you come from?' I asked him. 'Over the Pass,' he said and, Monsieur, the more I look at him the more I believe him. He's down in the hall now."

"Well, I'll come and see him but I don't believe that story about coming over the Pass. It must have been terrible up there last night."

When they reached the hall Lucien lay in a dead faint on the floor.

Monsieur Givet picked him up in his arms. "Bring a hot water bottle and some brandy and coffee to my room as quickly as possible," he said to the alarmed porter.

Upstairs he laid the boy on his bed, removed his sodden boots and socks and rubbed his numb feet. Then he took off his outer clothes and wrapped him in blankets. By this time the night porter had arrived with the hot water bottle, the brandy and the coffee.

The doctor held a spoonful of brandy to Lucien's lips. He did not open his eyes but gave a tired sigh and swallowed the brandy. When he opened his eyes a few minutes later he looked straight up into a kind face and couldn't think where he was.

"Who are you?" he murmured sleepily.

Monsieur Givet didn't answer immediately but raised Lucien's head and fed him slowly with hot coffee.

"I'm Monsieur Givet. I understand you wanted to see me."

"Are you a great, clever, famous doctor?"

"No, I'm just a doctor."

"Can you make lame children walk?"

"It depends why they're lame. Sometimes I can."

"He fell off a precipice and

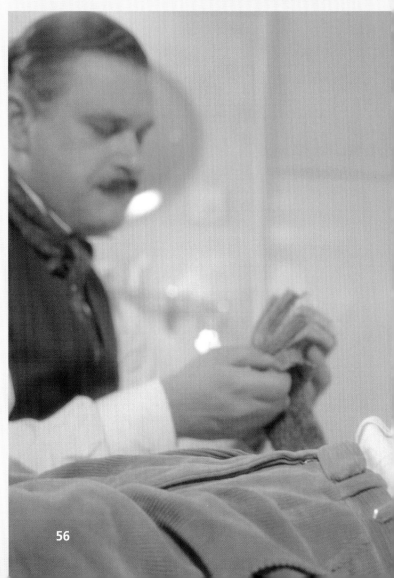

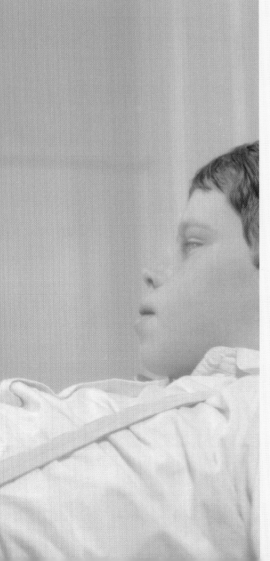

now he has to walk with crutches."

"Who does?" asked a bewildered Monsieur Givet.

"Little Dani Burnier. He lives in the chalet next to mine. So I came to ask whether you can make him well again. I've got enough money to pay you."

"How did you get here?"

"I came over the Pass on my skis."

"You can't have done - not in that blizzard."

"But I did; there's no other way to come."

Monsieur Givet stared at the boy as though he had come from another planet. Lucien reached inside his shirt and pulled out the fat stocking.

"Please, sir, is this enough money?" he asked.

Monsieur Givet emptied the stocking and gave a cry of astonishment.

"My boy, before we go any further you must tell me where this money came from. Do you know how much there is?"

"No, but my sister said you'd want a lot. Isn't it enough?"

"That depends whether you want to buy my clinic as well! Where did you get it from?"

"An old man I'm friends with gave it to me and there was a message. He said it was the payment of a debt - and you were to take it all," Lucien murmured sleepily.

"Who was this old man? Where does he live?" persisted the doctor.

"Please, he made me promise not to tell you..." Lucien's eyes closed; he was fast asleep.

After Lucien had fallen asleep, the porter brought a worried Marie to see Monsieur Givet.

"Oh sir," she cried, "Porter tells me you've got my little brother. Is he all right? We thought he must be dead in a snowdrift."

Monsieur Givet tried to get some sense out of her about Dani but she was too upset and only wanted to get away and tell her mother that Lucien was safe.

When Lucien at last woke up, Monsieur Givet tried to get more information out of him about the old man and the money but Lucien repeated that he had promised not to tell anything about him. Then he asked about Dani and how the accident had happened. Lucien went very red but he told the truth about teasing Dani and then dropping the kitten by mistake and Dani going after it.

"Since then he's never walked properly - only with crutches - and I thought perhaps..." his voice trailed off miserably.

"Lucien, it may be that God is going to make you the means of curing Dani," Monsieur Givet said gently. "I think he must have been looking after you in a very special way last night when you came over the Pass."

After they had eaten, Monsieur Givet and Lucien set off in the train and Monsieur Burnier met them at the station in the cart. All the villagers came to their doors as they passed because they had heard the story about Lucien's brave journey over the Pass.

At the Burniers' chalet Grandmother, Annette and Dani were all sitting in a row,

dressed in their best clothes, when the famous doctor arrived.

The doctor sat at the other end of the room from them and held out a sweet for Dani. Dani hopped delightedly across the room and the doctor watched him closely. Then he lifted him on to his lap and talked to him.

"Does your leg hurt?"

"No... only sometimes when I walk without my crutches."

Monsieur Givet watched Dani limping and then he laid him flat on the table and turned his leg this way and that.

"Well? Can you do anything for him?" asked Grandmother.

The doctor turned to Dani. "Where's that fine cat gone? Can you go and fetch her for me?"

After Dani had left the room, Monsieur Givet turned to Papa. "I think I may be able to help you, though I'd have to see an X-ray first.

I think the bone was not properly set and that I could break it again and straighten it. But it would mean an operation and a long stay in the hospital. Would you be willing to let him come?" Papa and Grandmother were worried about the money for the operation but Dr Givet assured them that there was nothing to pay. It was decided that Annette would go with Dani and help to look after him in the hospital. Dani was so excited at the prospect of a train journey with Annette that he didn't really think about the hospital.

"I'll see you at the station at half-past eight tomorrow morning," Monsieur Givet said as he left the chalet.

Monsieur Givet called at Lucien's chalet to see if they could direct him to where the old man lived.

"Oh yes, that would be the old man up the mountain who teaches Lucien wood carving," said Marie. She pointed out the path to him but warned him that the snow would be very deep.

Monsieur Givet thought how beautiful the forest looked as he toiled up the track. When he arrived at the old man's chalet, he found him hunched over his bench, carving.

"Well, did you get there safely, Lucien?" the old man asked, without looking up.

"It's not Lucien," said the doctor. The old man jumped and then they stared at each other for a long time. "I've come to give you back this money and to take you home, Father. We've missed you and wanted you."

So Monsieur Givet collected a sleigh and told Lucien about his father. Together they went to fetch the old man from his chalet.

Months passed and Annette wrote to Grandmother and Papa about Dani's good progress in the hospital. Grandmother always got Lucien to read the letters aloud to her when he came to help chop wood or get shopping for her. At last news came that Dani was well again and they were coming home.

It was a lovely spring morning when Papa and Grandmother went off to the station in the cart to meet the train. Lucien walked there slowly on his own, thinking again about the day just over a year ago when Dani had fallen. It had been his fault that they had to go away and perhaps they wouldn't be very pleased to see him.

He reached the station and stood apart from the others, feeling nervous and wishing he hadn't come.

"The train's coming!" cried Papa, and suddenly it was there. Annette and Dani were at the window, calling excitedly.

Dani glanced at the well-loved faces who had come to meet him and he noticed Lucien standing apart. He wanted to gather everyone about him and he jumped off the train and ran straight to Lucien.

"Look, Lucien," he shouted, "I can walk! The doctor you found made me better! Look, Papa!"

The family hugged each other. Lucien turned away with tears in his eyes because he had been singled out and the wrong he had done had been forgiven and forgotten for ever.

Spring had come - the winter was over and gone. With the flowers appearing and the birds singing again, joy had returned to their hearts.